FOR
MILES PARSONS AND HIS MOM AND DAD,
SAVITRI AND JON:
MAY WE ALWAYS REMEMBER.
—NL

IN MEMORY OF MY GRANDPARENTS
—RL

Little, Brown and Company

Hachette Book Group
1290 Avenue of the Americas, New York, NY 10104
Visit our website at www.lb-kids.com

Little, Brown and Company is a division of Hachette Book Group, Inc.
The Little, Brown name and logo are trademarks of Hachette Book Group, Inc.

The publisher is not responsible for websites (or their content) that are not owned by the publisher.

First Edition: December 2013

Library of Congress Cataloging-in-Publication Data • Laden, Nina. • Once upon a memory / written by Nina Laden; illustrated by Renata Liwska. — First edition. • pages cm • Summary: "A journey through the various cycles of growing up, from a garden that began as a single seed to a child remembering that he was once small"— Provided by publisher. ISBN 978-0-316-20816-1 • [1. Growth—Fiction. 2. Memory—Fiction.] I. Liwska, Renata, illustrator. II. Title. PZ7.L13735On 2013 • [E]—dc23 • 2012043086

10 9 8 7 6

APS

Printed in China

ABOUT THIS BOOK

The art was initially sketched by hand in the artist's journal. It was then scanned and colored in Adobe Photoshop. The animal characters were inspired by the artist's experiences with nature, from her worldwide travels to her own backyard.

This book was edited by Connie Hsu and designed by Alison Impey under the art direction of Patti Ann Harris. The production was supervised by Charlotte Veaney, and the production editor was Wendy Dopkin.

The text was set in Garamond.

Once Upon a Memory

Written by Nina Laden
Illustrated by Renata Liwska

Little, Brown and Company
New York Boston

Does a **feather** remember
it once was...

...a bird?

Does a **book** remember
it once was...

...a word?

Does a **chair** remember
it once was...

...a tree?

Does a **garden** remember
it once was...

...a pea?

Does a **cake** remember
it once was...

...grain?

Does an **ocean** remember
it once was...

. . . rain?

Does a **statue** remember
it once was...

...stone?

Does an **island** remember
it once was...

. . . unknown?

Does **work** remember
it once was...

...play?

Does **night** remember
it once was...

...day?

Does **love** remember
it once was...

. . . new?

Does a **family** remember
it once was...

...two?

Does the **world** remember
it once was...

. . . wild?

Will **you** remember
you once were...

...a child?

SOME OF OUR FAVORITE THINGS TO REMEMBER:

Eating Grandma's chocolate chip cookies

Learning to ski

Painting pictures with my mom

Making my first book by myself

Playing with my baby brother

Making my first best friend

Finding a fossil

Learning to speak French

Spending countless hours drawing my own world in my room

Eating jelly at Grandma's

Sitting by the bonfire and listening to stories

Canoeing for cattails with my dad on summer vacations

Listening to sounds while lying on the beach

Having houseguests and getting to stay up late

Getting letters and postcards from the mailbox

Searching for chocolates or candies

What are some of *your* favorite things to remember?